ROGER THE W.RASSE

AND THE ITCHY FISHES

To Mum, Dad, Tracey and Jodie xo
And a special thanks to Di Kelly and Geoff Johnston - S.P.

Little Pink Dog Books
PO Box 2039, Armidale, New South Wales 2350, Australia
www.LittlePinkDogBooks.com

A Catalogue-In-Publication entry for this book is available from the National Library of Australia.

ISBN: 978-0-6486528-5-4

A catalogue record for this book is available from the National Library of Australia

ROGER THE WRASSE
AND THE ITCHY FISHES

By
Dr Sue Pillans aka Dr Suzie Starfish

LITTLE PINK DOG BOOKS
Australia

Roger the wrasse is one of the smallest fish in the sea, but he has one of the BIGGEST jobs.

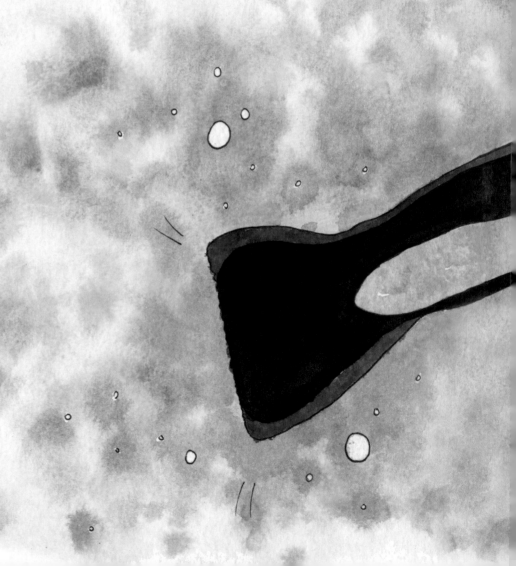

Every day Roger swims to a special part of the ocean where
his very important job takes place.
It is one of the busiest places on the reef.

Roger loves his work. He hums a tune as he sings his morning song:
'I've got my bucket and I'll need this broom.
My job is great as I'm here to groom.'

As Roger begins his daily dance, he announces in his BIGGEST voice:
'My cleaning service is pretty great,
So get in line and don't be late!'

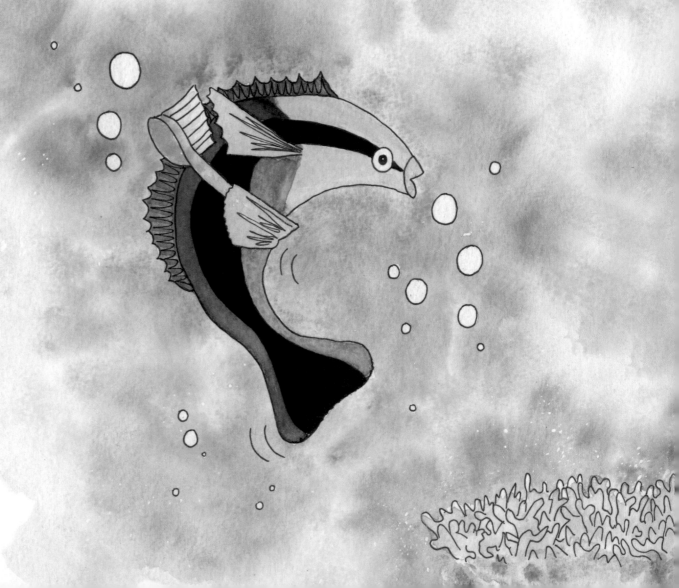

Roger opens up his station to all those in need.

Then, one by one, the visitors arrive ... lining up just to see Roger.

The first and BIGGEST fish approaches. This is the most
dangerous part of Roger's job, as he thinks out loud:
'For Stan, I'll need a ladder and a mop.
I'll have to scramble to get to the top.'

A BIG dark shape appears from above.
Grabbing his sponge
Roger swims towards
it, softly saying:
'In glides Michelle
with a bit of a frown,
So I end up
cleaning her
upside down!'

Next in line has scutes instead of scales.
So Roger grabs his BIGGEST bucket and BIGGEST brush,
calling out:
'Toby's so dirty ... and what is that smell!
I'll scrub and scrub for a shiny shell.'

It's almost closing time when out of the shadows slithers the last in line. With a fright,
Roger reaches for his broom, uttering in a shaky voice:

'Erica is slippery and looks really mean,
But it's my job to wash her and get her clean.'

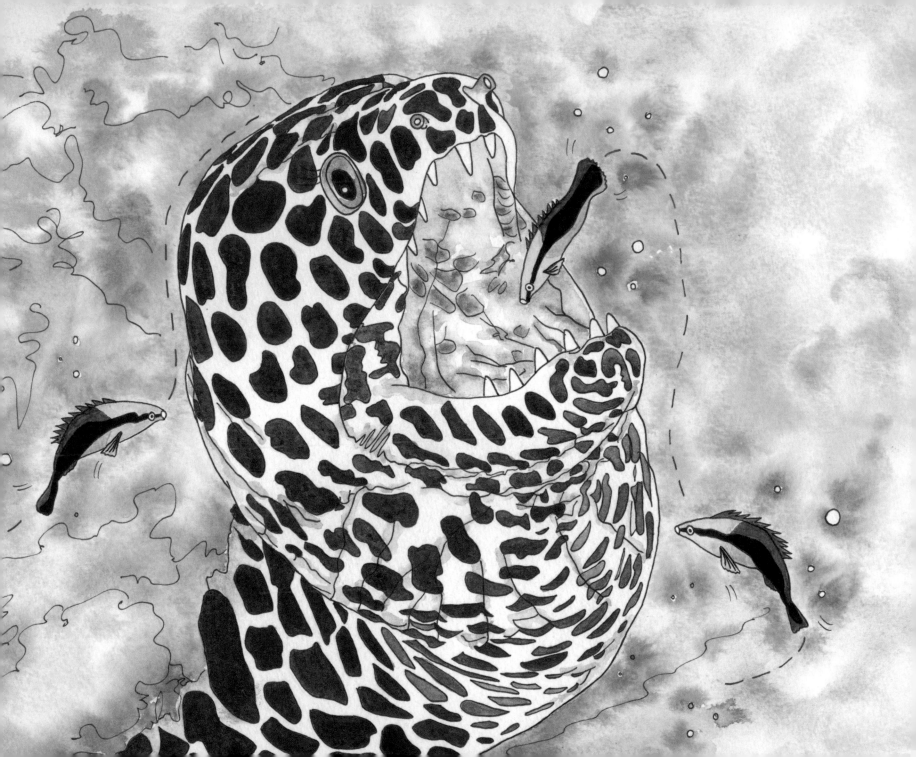

Roger swims in and out and all about. Until ... **SNAP!**
'Oh!'
GULP!!

Out of the darkness, Roger squeals:
'Please don't make me your next meal!
I'm here to help you, that's our deal!'

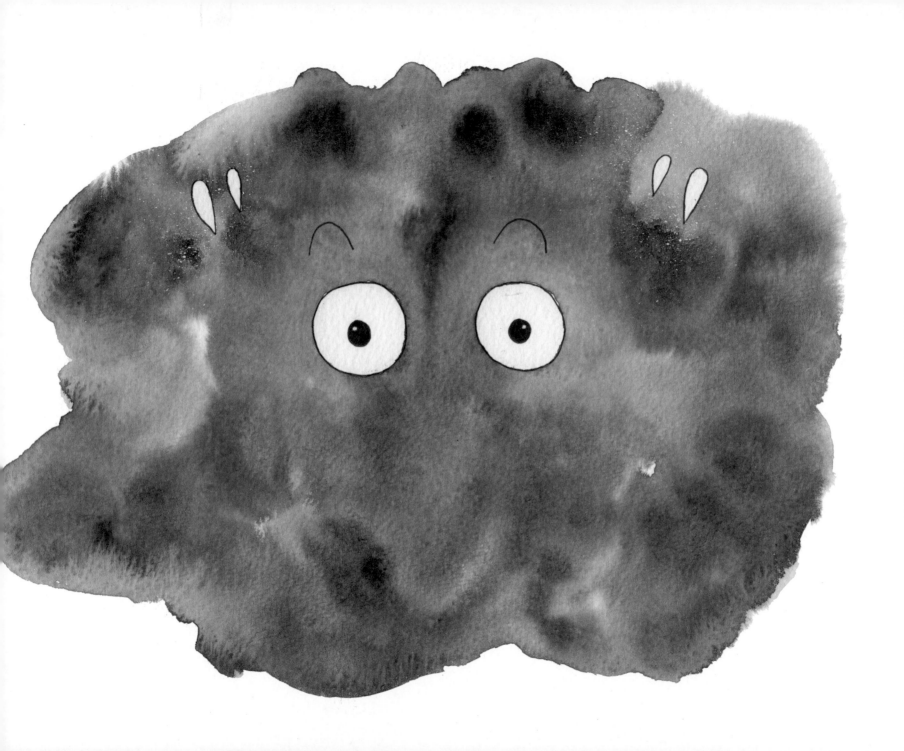

Shouting in his BIGGEST voice ever, Roger calls:

'Removing your itches is how I eat.

We can help each other, which is pretty neat.'

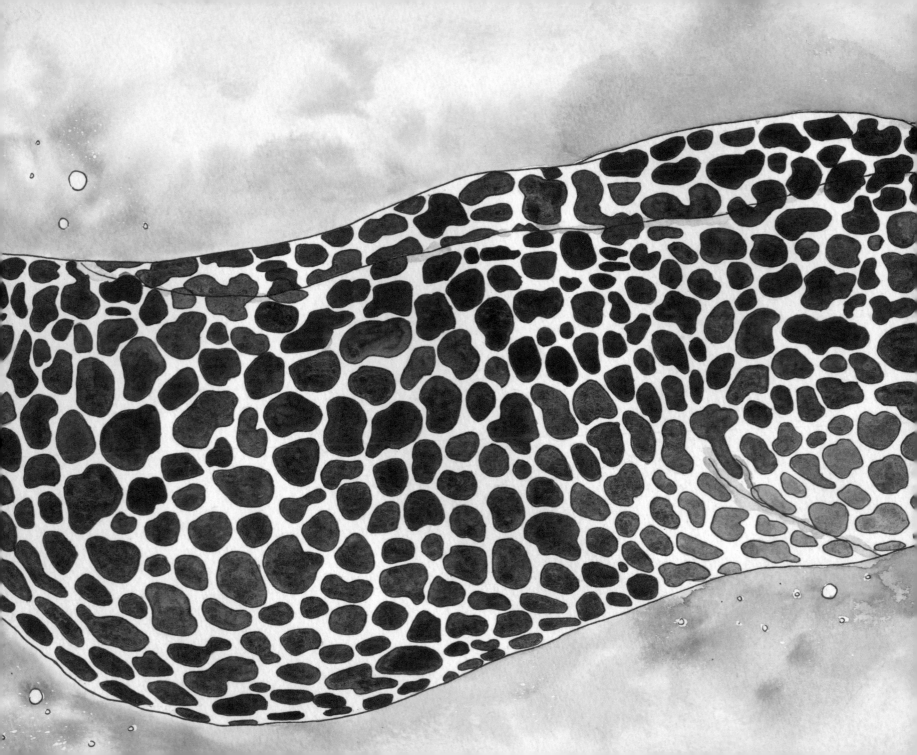

'Sorry, mate.
You're doing great,' says Erica.

After a BIG day of cleaning, Roger the wrasse packs up his bucket and mop, his broom and brush, and waves goodbye to his friends, the cleanest fishes on the reef ...

... and swims away quickly as they smile back.

UNDERWATER WONDERS

ABOUT CLEANING STATIONS

Cleaning stations are areas on the reef where fish, sharks, manta rays, moray eels and sea turtles gather to be cleaned. Cleaner wrasse, like Roger, remove parasites, dead skin cells and bacteria from the gills, flesh and mouths of fish and the bodies of marine animals. This is a very special relationship as cleaner fish provide a cleaning service to their 'clients' and in return, the cleaners get a full stomach. This is a great example of *mutualism* where two animals of different species are in a relationship where both benefit. So let's celebrate all of the small creatures that do BIG things in the ocean showing us you are never too small to make a BIG difference!

Best fishes,
Dr Suzie Starfish